Ladybug Girl
at the Beach

by David Soman and Jacky Davis

SCHOLASTIC INC.
New York Toronto London Auckland
Sydney Mexico City New Delhi Hong Kong

To Joanne McParland, beach lover and midwife

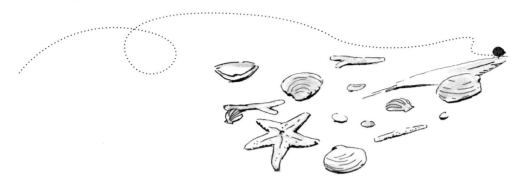

ISBN 978-0-545-37289-3

12 11 10 9 8 7 6 5 4 3 2 1   11 12 13 14 15 16/0

Printed in the U.S.A.   87

First Scholastic printing, May 2011

Designed by Teresa Dikun and Jasmin Rubero
Text set in Aunt Mildred

"We're finally here!" declares Lulu as she jumps out of the car and spreads her wings.

"I love the beach!" says Lulu.
"You've never even been to the beach before,"
  replies her big brother.
"But I already know that I love it," she says.
"And I can't wait to go swimming in the waves!"

The sand feels warm under her feet as Lulu and Bingo
lead the family to a good spot to spread their blanket.

Lulu runs to the edge of the water.

The ocean goes on and on, and makes huge roaring sounds.

She had no idea it was going to be so big and noisy.

She takes a few steps backward. Bingo barks at the waves.

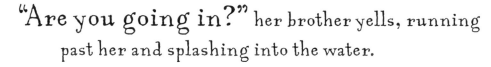

"Are you going in?" her brother yells, running past her and splashing into the water.

"I don't think so," she says.

"Um . . . I really came here to build sand castles."

Lulu retreats to the beach blanket to find her trusty pail and shovel.

She builds a giant sand castle, and uses little sticks
for people. The King and the Queen are very happy here,
she thinks. Bingo digs a moat to keep them extra safe.

Lulu walks over and sits down next to her mama.
She looks out at the ocean, which is glittering with
light. She thinks it looks pretty from far away.
"Do you want to go in the water?" asks Mama.
"No," Lulu says, "I want to fly the kite now."

Soon the kite is darting back and forth
in the wind, but Lulu holds on tight.

After the wind dies down, it feels really hot.
Lulu glances at the ocean.
She thinks the water would be cool,
but the waves still look much too big.

This is a good time to
remind her parents about ice cream.

Lulu lists all her top eleven favorite flavors:

"Chocolate Marshmallow, Cherry Vanilla, Pistachio,

Butter Pecan, Peppermint Bon Bon,

Peanut Butter Chip,

Raspberry Swirl,

Peach Pie,

Almond Fudge,

Royal Banana Surprise,

and . . .

Vanilla."

At the ice cream stand Lulu can't just choose one.
"This is a day for a double scoop," her mama says.
Sometimes mamas can be very right.

"Come on, Bingo," says Lulu
after she finishes her ice cream.
"Let's take a walk down the beach!"

~They find a long piece of driftwood.
Lulu writes loopy L's in the sand, and draws pictures of Bingo.
He's the perfect subject, and stays really still.

It is very hot. Lulu looks at the ocean.
Other kids are splashing and jumping in the waves.

She walks down to the edge of the water.
"Should we get our feet wet, Bingo?" she asks.
She thinks it would be okay to go into the ocean
just a little bit.

Suddenly a wave crashes into her
legs and nearly knocks her over.

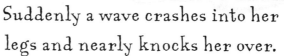

Just as she gets her balance
the whirling water races back and tries to
pull her in. Her feet get buried in the
sand up to her ankles.

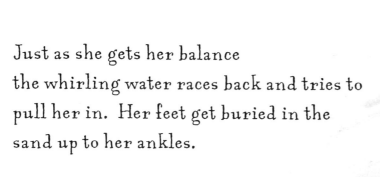

"Are you okay, Bingo?" Lulu asks.
She looks around to see if anyone noticed
that they were almost carried away,
but everyone is playing just as they were before.

"Let's be explorers!" says Lulu, brushing the sand off her knees. "We can collect things for our museum." They march off across the beach. They hear seagulls that sound like they are laughing,

discover little crabs that burrow into the sand,

and pick up slimy seaweed washed up on shore.

There are also lots of shells on the beach,
all different shapes and sizes.
She chooses the most special ones
and puts them into her pail.

"I know, Bingo! I bet if we dig, we could find a
pirate treasure!" says Lulu. She digs, and digs,
and digs. Finding treasure is hard work.

When Lulu feels the water splash against her,
she spins around. The tide has come in!
It is taking away her favorite pail!
She has to rescue it or it will be lost forever!

This is a job for Ladybug Girl!

"I'll save you!" she says, snapping up the pail.
When she looks down she realizes she is in the ocean.
She is actually **in** the ocean!
The water is past her knees, and she isn't afraid at all!

"Ladybug Girl isn't afraid of anything!"

For the rest of the long afternoon,
Ladybug Girl and Bingo splash in the water
and run on the beach daring the waves to catch them.

"You can't get me, waves.
I'm Ladybug Girl!"

Ladybug Girl and Bingo play until
the bright blue sky turns pink.
They make footprints in the sand.
At least 14 miles of them, Ladybug Girl thinks.
Every time the ocean erases them, they make more.

Then it is time to go, and Ladybug Girl
trudges back across the still-warm sand.
Bingo follows slowly, dragging his ears.

Standing at the top of the dunes,
Ladybug Girl waits for her brother.

"So, did you like your first time at the beach?"
    he asks.
"Yes," she answers.
"I told you, Ladybug Girl loves the beach!"